Gertrude and Toby Meet the Wolf

Book 3 in the Gertrude and Toby Fairy-Tale Adventure Series

Gertrude and Toby Meet the Wolf

Shari Tharp

art by Jim Heath

ATLAS PUBLISHING
Solana Beach, California

Gertrude and Toby Meet the Wolf

Written by Shari Tharp
Illustrated by Jim Heath
Text and illustrations copyright © 2016 Shari Tharp

Published by ATLAS PUBLISHING Solana Beach, California 92075
www.atlaspublishing.biz

Permissions, requests, and correspondence may be directed to the publisher at PO Box 1730, Solana Beach, CA 92075, or to permissions@atlaspublishing.biz.

Library of Congress Control Number: 2016956004

ISBN-13: 978-0-9969679-7-6

1 3 5 7 9 8 6 4 2

✼

This first edition printed in the United States of America

Gertrude and Toby Meet the Wolf

Design and layout by ATLAS PUBLISHING, Solana Beach, California

Composed in Jungle Juice, IM FELL FRENCH CANON, and Lustria

The art for this book consists of hand-drawn pencil illustrations on drafting vellum, subsequently colored and laid out using Adobe Photoshop and InDesign

For Sara-Ashley

ST

Dad—
Thanks for teaching
me to be an artist.

JH

Gertrude and Toby are best friends and live at McFarland Farms. Every Friday when Farmer Sam goes shopping in town, Gertrude and Toby sneak off the farm for a fun adventure.

This Friday, they have decided to go fishing at Trout Lake.

"Worms are the best bait," announced Gertrude.

"I declare, beetles are better!" said Toby.

"Behhh," said Gertrude. "You use your beetles and I'll use my worms. Whoever catches the most fish, wins."

"Wins what?" asked Toby.

"The winner gets to pick our next Friday adventure," said Gertrude.

"Indeed!" said Toby.

As soon as Farmer Sam's
truck rumbled through the front
gate, Gertrude and Toby set off
for Trout Lake.

They were walking along, when suddenly a boy
raced past them. "A wolf! A wolf is coming!" he cried.

Gertrude and Toby dove into the bushes. They waited and waited, but no wolf passed. So they crept out of the bushes and continued on.

Gertrude and Toby were almost to Trout Lake when the same boy jumped out from behind a tree. "A wolf! A wolf is coming!" he shouted.

Gertrude and Toby hid once more. They waited and waited, but again no wolf passed.

"Behhh, that's strange," said Gertrude.

"Indeed," whispered Toby.

Is there really a wolf? they wondered.

Gertrude and Toby finally arrived at Trout Lake. They set about looking for beetles and worms. Then they each picked out a cattail and made a fishing pole.

They began their fishing contest. Soon Toby had four fish, and Gertrude had only two.

"I do believe I am winning," Toby announced.

"Behhh! Not for long," said Gertrude as she felt a tug on her line.

Just then, they heard a shout. "Help me! Help me! Don't let him eat me!"

The boy who had cried wolf was being dragged down the dirt lane by the wolf himself!

Gertrude looked at Toby. "Are you thinking what I'm thinking?"

"That beetles are better bait than worms?" answered Toby.

"Behhh! No," said Gertrude, "let's help him!"

"I don't know . . . ," said Toby. "Wolves are very scary creatures."

Gertrude frowned at Toby. Then off she trotted after the wolf.

Toby grabbed their fish. "Wait for me!" he shouted.

Gertrude and Toby watched as the wolf pulled the boy into his cave. The wolf tied the boy's arms and legs with rope.

"Everybody knows that pigs are my favorite food," they heard the wolf say, "but I haven't been able to find any lately. I'm gonna make me some little-boy stew instead."

The wolf started a fire. "I'll be back," he growled.

While the wolf was busy collecting ingredients for his stew, Gertrude and Toby snuck into his cave. They took turns chewing through the rope. At last, the boy was free! Gertrude, Toby, and the boy ran from the wolf's cave as fast as they could go.

Suddenly, they heard a mighty growl. "Come back here with my lunch!"

They raced down the dirt lane! They hadn't gone far, when through the bushes, Gertrude spotted a red brick house.

"Over there!" she yelled.

They banged on the door.

KNOCK–KNOCK–KNOCK!

"Let us in, let us in—there's a wolf after us!" they cried.

"Not by the hair of our chinny chin chins!" came the reply.

"Please, please, let us in!" they shouted once more.

The door slowly opened. Out peeked three little pigs. The wolf ducked behind the bushes as Gertrude, Toby, and the boy dashed into the house.

Pigs! thought the wolf, and his mouth began to water. *I need a plan*, he thought. *A sure way to get a piglet for lunch.*

The hungry wolf made himself a disguise. Then he set off for the red brick house.

KNOCK–KNOCK–KNOCK!

"Mr. Lobo here! Selling my special soaps. Five for three dollars. On sale today!" he called out.

The first little pig peeked out the window. He saw the wolf's tail sticking out of his forest-made clothing.

"Oh no!" he gasped. "You've led the wolf straight to our front door!"

"No soap needed today, sir!" shouted the second little pig as he wiped mud from his brother's back.

The three little pigs stared at their visitors.
Gertrude thought fast. "We have fish!" she said. "I'm
sure the wolf would like some fish."

"You better hope so," said the third little pig, "or we'll toss out the turtle. Turtle soup can be mighty tasty."

"I declare," squeaked Toby, "I'm a tortoise!"

Gertrude called out, "Mr. Wolf, we know it's you. We have some tasty fish! We will give you our fish if you spare us."

"How many fish have you got?" growled the wolf.

"Six!" yelled Gertrude.

"Fine, I'll take the fish," said the wolf.

"And you'll go away?" asked Gertrude.

"Yes," said the wolf. "For today . . . ," he whispered under his breath.

Gertrude opened the window and tossed out the fish. Then she slammed the window shut.

"Whew!" said the three little pigs.

"Behhh!" went Gertrude.

"I declare!" said Toby.

"There really was a wolf!" said the boy. "Who knew?"

Gertrude and Toby waited. Then they waited a bit longer to be sure that Mr. Wolf was indeed gone.

When they decided it was safe to leave, they bade farewell to the boy and the three little pigs.

As they headed for home, Gertrude asked Toby, "Are you thinking what I'm thinking?"

"That I won our fishing contest?" answered Toby.

"Behhh! No," said Gertrude, "that we need to hurry. Farmer Sam will be home soon."

And off they ran to McFarland Farms.

Later that night, as Gertrude and Toby settled into the hay and were drifting off to sleep, Toby whispered, "I choose exploring the haunted forest as our next Friday adventure . . ."

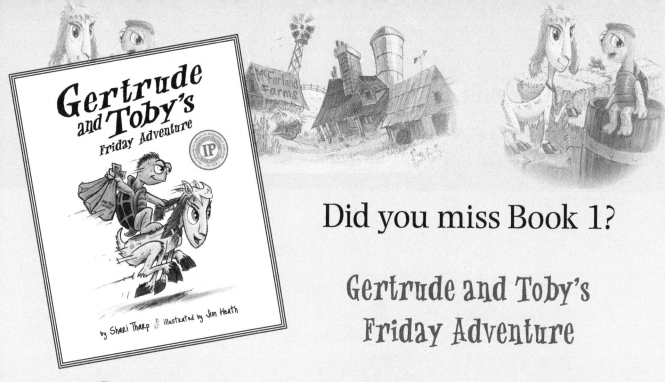

Did you miss Book 1?

Gertrude and Toby's Friday Adventure

Gertrude the goat and her best friend Toby the tortoise are adventurers. No sitting around on the boring farm for them! They love to explore, and every Friday they sneak off the farm for some extra fun. One Friday, Gertrude and Toby decide to visit the local candy store in town. They discover yummy goodies and treats, but soon find that the treats are not free!? Uh oh! The market owner grabs Toby. He demands money for the candy that Gertrude and Toby have taken by mistake. Gertrude must find a way to save her friend and get back home before Farmer Sam returns.

2016 Independent Publisher Book Awards (IPPY) Silver Medal Winner Best Children's Illustrated E-Book

"This delightful and entertaining volume is . . . very highly recommended for elementary school and community library collections [and] personal reading lists."

—*Midwest Book Review*

Find it at a retailer near you, or visit www.gertrudeandtoby.com.

Or Book 2?

Gertrude and Toby Save the Gingerbread Man

Gertrude and Toby are best friends and live at McFarland Farms. When farmer Sam and his son Ryan take their prize pig to the county fair, Gertrude and Toby decide they have plenty of time to sneak off the farm. While on their adventure, they discover that a giant has captured their friend, the Gingerbread Man! They come up with a plan to save him, but the giant, who is sleeping nearby, wakes up during their rescue.

Find it at a retailer near you, or visit www.gertrudeandtoby.com.

CPSIA information can be obtained
at www.ICGtesting.com
Printed in the USA
LVOW06*1410060217
523122LV00005B/8/P